FairyRealm

BOOK 4

The Last
fairy-apple Tree

ALSO BY EMILY RODDA

FAIRY REALM
The Charm Bracelet
The Flower Fairies
The Third Wish
The Magic Key
The Unicorn

ROWAN OF RIN
Rowan of Rin
Rowan and the Travelers
Rowan and the Keeper of the Crystal
Rowan and the Zebak
Rowan of the Bukshah

Fairy Realm

The Last Fairy-apple Tree

BOOK 4

EMILY RODDA

ILLUSTRATIONS BY RAOUL VITALE

HARPERCOLLINS*PUBLISHERS*

The Last Fairy-Apple Tree

Text copyright © 2000 by Emily Rodda

Illustrations copyright © 2003 by Raoul Vitale

www.harperchildrens.com

Library of Congress Cataloging-in-Publication Data

Rodda, Emily.

The last fairy-apple tree / Emily Rodda ; illustrations by Raoul Vitale. — 1st American ed.

p.   cm. — (Fairy realm ; book 4)

Sequel to: The third wish.

Summary: Jessie travels back to the magical world of the Realm to try to discover what has gone wrong in the Hidden Valley where the gnomes live and the fairy-apples grow.

ISBN 0-06-009592-X — ISBN 0-06-009593-8 (lib. bdg.)

[1. Gnomes—Fiction. 2. Apples—Fiction. 3. Magic—Fiction.] I. Vitale, Raoul, ill. II. Title.

PZ7.R5996Las2003   2002038800

[Fic]—dc21   CIP

                                                          AC

Typography by Karin Paprocki

8 9 10

❖

First American Edition

Previously published by ABC Books for the

AUSTRALIAN BROADCASTING CORPORATION

GPO Box 9994 Sydney NSW 2001

Originally published under the name

Mary-Anne Dickinson as the Storytelling Charms Series 1995

CONTENTS

Fairy Realm

BOOK 4

The Last Fairy-apple Tree

granny's problem

"The fairy-apple trees," murmured Jessie's grandmother. The charm bracelet on her wrist jingled softly as she lifted her hand to touch the painting on the wall in front of her.

She glanced at Jessie's curious face and smiled, her green eyes twinkling as they always did when she spoke about magic things.

"I haven't told you about that part of the Realm, have I, Jessie?" she said. "About Hidden Valley, and the gnomes, and the fairy-apple trees?"

Jessie stood in the pool of morning sunlight that streamed through the window of the spare bedroom at Blue Moon and watched her grand-mother's slim fingers trace the outlines of the trees in the painting.

"Fairy-apple trees!" she exclaimed. "Are they where fairy-apple jelly comes from?"

Her mouth watered as she thought about fairy-apple jelly. It was one of her favorite things in all the world: a clear, sweet, golden pink jelly you spread on fresh bread.

Granny had made fairy-apple jelly for as long as Jessie could remember. She made it from fruit she gathered from a neighbor's tree. And in winter, small, glistening jars of it were always lined up on a shelf in the Blue Moon pantry.

Jessie's mother, Rosemary, always said that "fairy-apple" was just Granny's name for ordinary apple jelly. But Jessie could see that the apples on the trees in the painting weren't ordinary. They were very small and round, and a beautiful gold-red color.

"I didn't know fairy-apples grew in the Realm too," she said.

Granny smiled dreamily. "Oh, that's where all

2

the fairy-apple trees grow," she said. "All but one."

Jessie leaned closer to her so that she wouldn't miss a single word. She knew how lucky she was. No one else on earth had a grandmother like hers.

Most days, life at Blue Moon was peaceful and ordinary. Jessie went to school, her mother went to work at the hospital, Granny cooked, gardened and shopped. Things were *so* peaceful and ordinary, in fact, that sometimes Jessie almost forgot that Blue Moon was a special place, and that Granny wasn't at all what she seemed.

She was a fairly unusual sort of grandmother, anyway. She laughed a bit more than most. She sang strange-sounding songs. She liked to walk in the rain. She talked to birds and flowers, and to her big ginger cat, Flynn.

She was so unusual that some people, like their next-door neighbors, the Bins family, thought she was crazy!

Granny wasn't crazy, of course. But she *was* different from other people.

And only Jessie knew just how different.

For only Jessie knew that Granny wasn't from the mortal world at all.

When Granny's eyes held that special spark of light and she talked, like this, of magic things, Jessie remembered her secret. Once, long ago, her grandmother had been a fairy princess. She had left her own world, the fairy world of the Realm, to marry the artist Robert Belairs, the human man she loved.

Jessie herself had had some amazing adventures in the Realm since she and Rosemary had first come to live with Granny at Blue Moon. The charms of Jessie's own bracelet were proof of that. Each one had been given to her by the Folk of the Realm, to remind her of her visits.

She knew a lot about the Realm by now. But she had never heard of the gnomes of Hidden Valley, or their fairy-apple trees.

Jessie looked at the painting Granny was touching. Jessie's grandfather, Robert Belairs, had painted it. Robert was dead now, but his paintings still glowed on the walls of Blue Moon. This one

4

was especially beautiful. It showed a misty valley where dozens of little gnomes swarmed among trees loaded with golden red fairy-apples. Baskets already piled high with the fruit stood on the green grass, ready to be taken away.

A beautiful woman with a gold band around her head and long hair the same golden red color as the fruit sat on the grass beneath one of the trees. She held a fairy-apple in her hand, and her lap was filled to overflowing.

"Is that you, Granny?" asked Jessie.

Granny nodded. "Long ago," she said. "I loved Hidden Valley as much as Robert did. When the fairy-apple trees bloom, there's no lovelier place in all the Realm. Not many Folk go there. Not many even know the way. But we did."

She sighed and looked at the painting again. Her hand dropped to her side.

"What's the matter?" Jessie asked. "Don't you feel well?"

"Oh—no . . . I'm fine." Granny glanced at her quickly and hesitated. Then she smiled. "You

5

always know how I'm feeling, don't you, Jessie?" she said. "I can't hide anything from you. We're too alike."

Twining around her ankles, Flynn the cat purred. Granny bent to stroke his head.

"It's like this," she said thoughtfully, frowning. "Lately, for some reason, I keep thinking about Hidden Valley. I keep getting pictures of the place in my mind. The gnomes' village. The fairy-apple trees. I keep wanting to come and look at this painting." She sighed. "I keep feeling that something's wrong."

"What could be wrong?" asked Jessie.

Granny frowned again. "That's the point," she said. "What *could* be wrong? The Hidden Valley gnomes are happy, hard-working people. A bit too fond of gold, maybe . . ."

She thought about that for a moment. "The Folk and the fairies laugh at them sometimes. They say the gnomes will do anything for money," she said. "But the gnomes work hard all year in the mountain gold mines, except at fruit-picking time. You can understand how they've come to

6

love gold so much."

She began to pace restlessly around the room, her eyes always straying back to the painting on the wall.

"I don't see how liking money too much could bring them trouble," said Jessie.

Granny shrugged. "I don't either, really," she said. "It might bring unhappiness to some. But trouble? No."

She clasped her hands. "Still, it's all I can think of, Jessie. The ogres and others who might want to harm the gnomes, or steal from them, can't get into the Realm."

"The hedge keeps them out." Jessie nodded. She knew all about the enchanted hedge that protected the Realm and its creatures.

"Yes," said Granny. "The hedge is as strong and healthy as it's ever been. And the Realm magic is powerful enough to keep it that way."

"So the trouble at Hidden Valley, if there *is* trouble, must be coming from *inside* the Realm itself," Jessie said. "How strange."

They stood in silence, while the sunlight in the

spare room grew brighter on the painting of the gnomes and the fairy-apple trees. Then Granny spoke.

"I could be imagining things, Jessie," she said. "But I don't think so. I live away from the Realm now, but I'm still its true Queen. I trust my feelings about it. And the more I think about it, the more I'm sure that there's trouble in Hidden Valley. I *must* find out what it is."

"So you're going to the Realm?" Jessie asked excitedly.

"No, I can't do that." Granny shook her head almost sadly. "I gave up my place in the Realm when I came to this world. My sister Helena is Queen there now. And I have to leave her alone to rule in peace."

"Then how can you find out what's wrong in Hidden Valley, Granny?" cried Jessie, very disappointed. "There's no point in just worrying and thinking about it. You have to *do* something!"

Her grandmother smiled at her pink, indignant face. "Oh, but I *am* going to do something, Jessie," she said.

wyldwood

Jessie clasped her hands in excitement. Her charm bracelet tinkled on her wrist and she looked down at it. Maybe she could add another charm to it soon. She wondered what it would be.

"We'll have to think of a good excuse for your visit," said Granny briskly, as if she was talking about something absolutely normal. "I don't want to frighten anyone, or have Helena think I'm interfering."

"Yes, Granny," Jessie said, trying to sound calm and grown-up.

"Fortunately your mother is in the city for the

11

weekend," Granny went on, "so if you have to be away overnight she won't be worried. It's not very far from the palace to Hidden Valley by the secret way, but I don't think I should expect you back at Blue Moon until tomorrow. Now. Are you ready?"

"Am I going now?" Jessie squeaked. "I haven't even had breakfast!"

Granny laughed. "Nothing worse than going off on an adventure with an empty stomach, is there?" she teased. "No, Jessie. I didn't mean you'd have to start off for the Realm straightaway. I want to show you something right here first."

They went out into the crisp, spring morning air. Granny led the way out of the Blue Moon front gate and down the winding street.

"Where are we going?" Jessie asked.

But Granny only smiled mysteriously and said, "Wait and see."

They stopped in front of a pretty little house with a green roof and the name "Wyldwood" on the door. It looked lonely and neglected. A large FOR SALE sign was tacked to the front fence, and the grass in the front garden was long and untidy.

Granny pushed open the gate.

"Is it all right for us to go in?" asked Jessie nervously.

"Why not?" Granny said as they walked down the front path. "The man who used to own this house let me visit, and I think that should hold until the place is sold, don't you?"

"Was he a friend of yours?" asked Jessie.

Granny began to move down the side of the house. Jessie followed. At the end of the path was a big back garden. It was filled with tangled blackberry bushes, drifts of sweet-smelling freesias, and blossoming, mossy apple and pear trees.

"Not exactly a friend," Granny said. "Old Lucas Saw didn't have friends. He didn't have time for them. He cared about nothing but making money—and more money. So he had no friends, no family, no pets, no fun. He lived in this beautiful place, and he never really saw it. All he thought about was a pile of banknotes in an old tin box. He lived alone, and he died alone. Poor Lucas Saw."

She sighed. "But if he wasn't really my friend, he *was* my neighbor." She pointed. "You see?

13

There's the Blue Moon garden there, behind the blackberry bushes. The Wyldwood garden backs onto it. Before the blackberries grew so wild, Lucas and I could talk over the fence. We used to trade. Once a year."

"Trade?" Jessie was bewildered.

"Yes," said Granny, leading the way through the thick grass. "Lucas had something I wanted. And he let me have it in return for something *he* wanted. Fresh eggs from my chickens. That's how trade works."

"What did he have that *you* wanted?" Jessie dodged a spiderweb and gazed around the overgrown garden. She couldn't see anything here that Granny could possibly need.

Granny was silent. Jessie turned back to her and saw that her face had fallen. Suddenly she looked very sad.

"Oh dear," she murmured. Tears had filled her green eyes.

"Granny, what is it?" begged Jessie. "What's wrong?"

"That," said Granny, pointing.

14

Jessie looked and saw a small fish pond, almost hidden in the grass. Its dark water was speckled with insects and flecks of bark from the twisted branches of an overhanging tree.

"Fish?" she asked in surprise.

Granny smiled sorrowfully. "Oh no, Jessie. If there ever were fish in that pond, they're long gone. No. The tree!"

Jessie raised her eyes to the strange little tree that leaned over the black water of the pond. There was nothing much to see. Its stubby, gnarled branches were stiff and dead-looking, and covered with silver-gray lichen. Thick grass and weeds grew high around its trunk.

"That's what I wanted to show you," said Granny softly. "I wanted you to see it blossoming. It's a fairy-apple tree. The only one in this world, as far as I know. It lived for fifty years. Six months ago I picked fruit from it. But now it's dead. Or very, very nearly." She bowed her head.

"Oh, how *awful*," cried Jessie. "But Granny, are you sure it's a fairy-apple tree? It doesn't look a bit like the ones in Grandpa's painting. They're tall and beautiful and . . ."

Granny shrugged. "In Hidden Valley fairy-apple trees grow from seed while you watch. They cover themselves with flowers and fruit while the birds that nest in them raise one family of chicks. They live one or two seasons. Then they die, and more trees grow like magic from the seeds in the fallen fruit. But in this world, it's different."

"How did the tree get here?" Jessie asked.

"When Robert took me away from the Realm over fifty years ago, he had two fairy-apples in his pocket," Granny said. "I think Patrice, my old nanny, had given them to him." She smiled at the memory, and Jessie smiled too, thinking of plump little Patrice, now the Realm palace housekeeper, and a good friend.

"Robert and I ate the fairy-apples when we arrived at Blue Moon," Granny went on. "I threw my core away, high into the air, without even thinking about it. But Robert planted his. He hoped fairy-apple trees would grow from the seeds, to remind me of home."

"And they did!" said Jessie.

Granny shook her head. "No. Nothing came of those carefully planted seeds. Robert was very disappointed. Perhaps if we had put them in soil from Hidden Valley, or I had planted the core myself, they might have grown. I don't know. But one day I looked across the fence into Wyldwood and saw—a little fairy-apple tree. The core I'd thrown away so carelessly had landed next door and one of the seeds had somehow sprouted and grown. We couldn't believe it!"

She looked fondly at the gnarled little tree in front of her. "Robert said that the magic on my fingers had helped it to grow. Magic was thick in the air, the day I left the Realm. Anyway, there it was."

She sighed. "It wasn't as tall and strong as the fairy-apple trees we remembered. And no new trees grew from the seeds it dropped. But it was a fairy-apple tree all the same. It gave me fruit every year. I'm sorry it's dead." She pressed her lips together to hold back the tears.

Jessie waded through the long grass and touched the strange tree's rough bark. She felt a tiny tingle on her fingertips. And something else. A feeling of sadness and alarm filled her. She spun round. "Granny!" she whispered.

Her grandmother was standing motionless. "You feel it too!" she said. Her green eyes, wet with tears, were alight with fear.

Jessie pulled her hand away from the tree, shaking it as if she'd been burned. She stepped sideways and banged her ankle, hard.

"Ow!" she yelled crossly. She bent, rubbing her ankle, and pulled at the weeds to see what had hurt her.

There, sitting on the edge of the pond, was a dirty, battered-looking stone figure. A garden gnome, holding a fishing rod. It had been completely hidden in the choking grass that had grown up around it.

"Oh, look!" Jessie called.

Granny barely glanced up. She was deep in thought.

Feeling rather dizzy, Jessie squatted down beside the gnome. Her hand still tingled. She bit her lip and made an effort to smile. "Caught anything?" she whispered, and rubbed the gnome's rusty red cap.

There was a cracking sound and a shimmer in the air. Startled, Jessie jumped, blinked, lost her balance and tripped over backward.

"Nothing at all!" said a squeaky voice. "But you should have seen the one that got away. Oh, by my gold, I'm stiff!"

And the garden gnome dropped his fishing rod, scratched his beard, and stood up!

CHAPTER THREE

Bilbert the Brave

Jessie screamed with fright.

Granny spun around and came running toward her. Then she stopped and her hand flew to her mouth. "What in the Realm . . ." she breathed.

The gnome looked up at her. His eyes widened and an amazed expression appeared on his face. Then he raised his arm, crossed it over his grubby chest and bowed low, so that his tangled beard swept the ground. "Your Majesty," he mumbled. "Your servant, Bilbert the Brave . . . ah . . . your servant, Bilbert the Brave, from Hidden Valley, presents his compliments, and . . ."

He straightened up, looking pale and ill. He stood swaying, staring at her, opening and closing his mouth. "I'm sorry," he managed to say at last. "Something . . . seems to . . . be . . ." And then his eyes rolled back in his head and he fell flat on the grass.

Jessie sat with Bilbert's head in her lap while Granny bathed his forehead with water from the fish pond.

"He'll be all right," said Granny. "He's just fainted. He's very weak."

"I'll bet he is," exclaimed Jessie. "After being turned to stone I'd be feeling very weak too!" She stared at the gnome, fascinated. "He looks just like an ordinary garden gnome," she said.

"Of course," Granny answered calmly. "Why do you think the plaster gnomes in people's gardens look the way they do?"

"I never thought about it," said Jessie.

"Well, it's because they're copied from the real thing," Granny said, still lightly stroking

Bilbert's dirty forehead.

"He's been here a while," she murmured. "Months, I'd say. He wasn't here when I came to pick the fairy-apples in autumn. But I wouldn't be surprised if he came very soon after that. It's no wonder he's feeling poorly." She clicked her tongue in irritation. "Dear oh dear—poor thing! These gnomes— If only they wouldn't leave the Realm! It's so *dangerous* for them."

"Why especially for gnomes?" asked Jessie. "The flower fairies come in and out without any trouble. And you're here all the time."

"Oh yes, but the flower fairies never stay long. And I'm one of the Folk. The worst thing that can happen to *us* is that we can lose our memories of the Realm. Well, you know that's why I wear this." She showed Jessie her charm bracelet.

Jessie nodded. She knew that the bracelet held Granny's Realm memories.

"But the gnomes are different," Granny went on. "If they come to this world in the daytime, they're fine. But if they stay too long, and get caught in moonlight—well, you saw what happened to Bilbert. They turn to stone and stay that way until someone with a bit of magic about them comes and rubs them on the head to set them free. And of course that means that some of them are never released at all."

Jessie squirmed. What a scary thought. She decided to rub the head of any garden gnome she came across from now on. Just in case.

"It was very lucky for Bilbert that we happened to come along when we did," said Granny. "And that you found him, under all that grass."

"Do you think Bilbert was the reason for your feeling about Hidden Valley?" asked Jessie.

"Maybe," said Granny slowly. "Although somehow . . ."

Bilbert stirred and groaned. His head rolled from side to side on Jessie's lap. He really was a mess, Jessie thought. His face and hands were filthy, his beard was matted and sticky with seeds and twigs, and moss was growing on his boots.

He opened his eyes. "Where am I?" he squeaked.

"Safe," said Granny firmly. "Now, can you stand up?"

Somehow Bilbert staggered to his feet. "Your Majesty," he began, wobbling on the spot. "Your servant—"

"Bilbert, don't start that again," Granny warned. "Jessie and I will help you home. We can talk there."

She leaned down and took hold of one of Bilbert's arms, and Jessie bent to take the other.

"Bilbert the Brave does *not* need help!" protested the gnome, insulted. He shook off their hands. "Bilbert the Brave . . ." He rocked back on his heels and nearly fell over again.

"Bilbert of Hidden Valley!" thundered Granny, drawing herself up and looking very queenly, despite her warm trousers and sensible shoes. "Make your decision! Will you let us help you home? Or do you want to stay here till moonrise and turn to stone again?"

After that, Bilbert saw he didn't have any choice. He allowed himself to be helped along quite meekly, glancing up at Granny's stern face now and then. Jessie was impressed. She didn't see her grandmother being serious and royal very often.

But by the time they reached the Wyldwood front gate, Bilbert was staggering and stumbling. It was clear that he didn't have the strength to walk to Blue Moon.

"We'll have to carry him," said Granny.

Bilbert's dirty face flushed bright pink with embarrassment. Being helped was bad enough, but being carried was terrible! "Bilbert the Brave . . ." he began, in a quavering voice.

Granny smiled at him. "Don't be ashamed, Bilbert," she said soothingly. "Don't forget, warriors injured in battle sometimes must be carried from the field."

Bilbert brightened up a lot now that he had been compared with a warrior. He let Granny pick him up in her arms without further trouble. She led the way out of the gate and started back up the hill.

"Couldn't we take turns carrying him, Granny?" asked Jessie, wanting to help.

26

"No—I think I had better do it," panted her grandmother. "He's heavier than he looks. And besides"—she winked at Jessie so that Bilbert couldn't see—"it's only right an injured warrior is carried by the most royal person present."

Bilbert beamed with pride.

They turned the corner. And there, coming down the hill toward them, were Irena Bins and her father.

"Oh no!" breathed Granny. "Not the Bins!"

"An enemy, Your Majesty?" exclaimed Bilbert, struggling in her arms. "Put me down. Let me at them, and I'll defend you!"

"You couldn't defend me against an angry gooseberry in your present state, Bilbert!" snapped Granny. "Lie absolutely still and say nothing. I command you!"

Bilbert froze, as if he had been turned back into stone.

"Act normally!" whispered Granny to Jessie, as Irena and Mr. Bins approached. "Pretend we're just having a stroll. They mustn't guess that

Bilbert's a real gnome. If they do, we'll really be in trouble. Before we know it there'll be TV cameras and scientists crawling all over Blue Moon. They might even stumble across the Door to the Realm. That would be a disaster!"

It wasn't very easy to act normally, with Granny staggering by her side under the weight of a large gnome. But Jessie did her best.

"Hi, Irena," she smiled cheerily, as Irena stopped, staring, in front of her.

"Hi," said Irena, shooting suspicious glances in Granny's direction. She nudged her father.

"You're out early, Mrs. Belairs," said Mr. Bins, his gaze fixed on Bilbert.

"Yes," answered Granny airily. "I love a walk before breakfast, don't you?"

Mr. Bins said nothing. He just stood there, plump and red-faced, blocking the path.

"Been down to Wyldwood?" he asked finally.

"We walked that way," said Granny. "Why?"

"Thought you might have been doing a spot of trespassing." Mr. Bins smiled, showing all his teeth, and wagged his finger in her face. "Don't think I don't know you go in there and pick fruit, Mrs. Belairs."

Granny drew herself up as best she could with Bilbert weighing her down. "Lucas Saw allowed me to," she said. "And—"

"That agreement ended when old Saw died," Mr. Bins interrupted. "I'm the agent in charge of Wyldwood. And I'm telling you, there's to be no more trespassing."

"If you're the agent in charge," said Granny, "I suggest you do something about the shocking state of the garden. Everything's dying."

"I'm not going to waste time or money on that sort of nonsense!" growled Mr. Bins. "Any more than Lucas Saw would have done."

"Poor Lucas," Granny murmured.

Mr. Bins snorted. "*Poor* Lucas? What rubbish. Lucas Saw died a very rich man."

Granny's mouth turned down at the corners. "Depends what you call rich," she said.

Mr. Bins' eyes narrowed. "And where did you

get *that*!" he demanded, pointing a fat finger at Bilbert. "Is that Wyldwood property?"

"Of course not!" Granny exclaimed indignantly. "Wyldwood property? Are you accusing me of *stealing*, Mr. Bins?"

His face went even redder. "Well, what are you doing with it, then?" he blustered. "What are you doing carrying round a garden gnome?"

"I'm taking it for a walk. It needs the exercise," said Granny calmly. "Now, Mr. Bins, please let us pass, Jessie and I would like to go home to have some breakfast."

CHAPTER FOUR

Into the Realm

"I don't know how it happened, Your Majesty," said Bilbert, with his mouth full of toast. "I don't even know why I was in that place. I can only remember eating a few fairy-apples—not many, five or six—and then deciding to fish for a while."

"You must have fallen asleep." Granny shook her head at him.

Bilbert pretended not to hear. He wiped his mouth with the back of his hand, and crumbs showered down into his beard to join all the leaves, twigs and seeds already stuck there.

Granny passed him a bowl of fresh pears. Bilbert took two, and Jessie stared. She'd never seen anyone so small eat so much. Or eat so greedily. Bilbert stuffed the food into his mouth as though he was starving, and took no notice of the mess he made. He crunched the pears whole, and seeds and bits of core fell into his beard and onto the tablecloth.

"You'll remember when you get back to Hidden Valley," Granny told him. Unlike Jessie, she didn't seem at all surprised by Bilbert's bad manners.

Bilbert stopped chewing. He cleared his throat. "One small problem . . ." he said, and looked embarrassed.

"You can't remember how to get back." Granny's eyes twinkled. "Well, that's to be expected, Bilbert. But as it happens, Jessie has been wanting to see Hidden Valley. The Door to the Realm is at the bottom of my garden. Jessie can take you through to the Realm and help you on from there."

She exchanged glances with Jessie, and Jessie understood. Of course! This gave her the perfect excuse to travel to Hidden Valley without having to say anything to anyone about Granny's worries.

"Well, I don't know . . ." The gnome puffed out his already stuffed cheeks and looked sideways at Jessie. You could tell Bilbert the Brave wasn't too pleased at the idea of being looked after by a little girl. He thought it was insulting.

"I mean—" Granny added, trying not to smile, "I would be so grateful if you would go with her on her journey—as a guard and protector."

"Oh! Well, then, of course, I would be happy to oblige, Your Majesty!" Bilbert's chest swelled under his grubby green coat. He swallowed the last piece of pear and jumped up from the table.

He bowed. "Your granddaughter will be quite safe with Bilbert the Brave, the strongest, cleverest, most heroic gnome in Hidden Valley." He turned to Jessie. "Your worries are over, little princess!"

"I'm not a princess," Jessie exclaimed indignantly. "And I wasn't worried. I've been to the Realm alone before. Lots of times."

She glared at Bilbert. He is *the* most conceited gnome I've ever met, she thought. Not that I've met one before. But all gnomes can't possibly be as bad as Bilbert. If they are, I'm not sure I *want* to go to Hidden Valley. Imagine a whole village full of Bilberts!

Granny winked at her. "Never mind, Jessie." She laughed. "I'm sure you and Bilbert will have a lovely time together. All will be well."

Jessie said nothing. She wasn't at all sure about that.

The secret garden was as peaceful as always. The hedge that grew around it seemed to keep the whole world out, and the smooth green grass was soft under Jessie's feet. The warm air was filled with the scent of rosemary.

The familiar feeling of excitement filled her. Soon she would be in the Realm. Soon she would be seeing her old friends—timid Giff the elf; Maybelle the bossy, miniature horse; and kind Patrice. And Queen Helena.

What adventures were in store for her this time? Her heart thudded.

She looked back through the door in the hedge to the old house nestling behind the tall trees that grew in the rest of the garden. "Good-bye, Blue Moon," she breathed. "I'll be back soon."

"Now," said Granny, putting her hand on Jessie's shoulder. "Remember all I've said. Queen Helena will arrange for you and Bilbert to be guided to Hidden Valley." She paused. "And take no risks, Jessie," she added. "Do you understand?"

Jessie nodded.

"There is no risk with Bilbert the Brave on guard!" said Bilbert loudly. As he spoke, his knees wobbled, and he clutched at Jessie's arm for support.

Jessie winced. He was heavy. And he was so *dirty*! That wasn't all his fault, of course. After all, he'd been sitting in the Wyldwood garden for months. But he hadn't even bothered to wash his face and hands or brush down his clothes before leaving Blue Moon. And now he had crumbs and bits of pear from breakfast tangled in his beard along with everything else. He's just a natural grub, Jessie thought in disgust.

"Just remember what you've been through, Bilbert," said Granny. "You can't expect to be quite yourself for a while yet."

"Look after him," she whispered in Jessie's ear as he turned away. "Don't let him think for a minute there might be a problem in Hidden Valley. It'll only frighten him. He's frightened enough already."

Jessie raised her eyebrows. Frightened? Bilbert, with his loud voice and conceited words, didn't seem to her to be afraid of anything.

As usual, Granny read her mind. "Don't be fooled by the act he puts on," she said softly. "He's scared to death. He'll be all right once he's home, but he's very weak now. Take care."

"I will, Granny," Jessie promised. She felt a bit ashamed of herself. Bilbert needed her help. He was lost and weak and, Granny had said, afraid. What did it matter if his beard wasn't brushed or his face wasn't clean?

She took his hand. "Let's go, then," she said.

Granny raised her head. "Open!" she commanded.

Jessie shut her eyes. She felt a whispering rush of cool air swirl around her as the magic Door opened. Her hair blew around her face. She heard

Bilbert gasp and his hand tightened in hers. Then she felt herself slipping, slipping away. Away from the secret garden and Granny and Blue Moon.

Into the Realm.

Jessie opened her eyes as the hedge closed, glossy and strong, behind her. The road, the grass and the trees of the Realm were just as she remembered them. Golden light, filled with twinkling flecks of magic, filled the air.

Bilbert took a deep breath. He beckoned to Jessie. "Forward, little princess!" he cried. "Follow me!"

He took three big steps along the road and fell over.

Jessie ran to pick him up.

He brushed her aside. "I'm fine, princess. Just tripped," he said.

Jessie had had enough. Magic was magic. But a bit of human common sense was needed here as well. She put her hands on her hips and stamped her foot.

"Now listen, Bilbert," she said. "For one thing,

my grandmother might be a queen, but I'm *not* a princess. Please call me Jessie. For another thing, you've got to stop dashing around and pretending you're all right. You've been turned to stone for months and months, and you're *not* all right. Who would be?"

Bilbert opened his mouth to protest but Jessie rushed on.

"And the last thing is, you're going the wrong way!" she snapped. "We have to go to the palace and see Patrice, the housekeeper. She's a friend of mine. She'll arrange for us to see Queen Helena. Now, please let me help you up. And then *you* follow *me*!"

The palace gleamed gold behind its screen of pale-leaved trees. Its great front door was firmly closed. But Jessie didn't want to go in that way. She led the stumbling Bilbert around to the side until they came to a small door.

Jessie knocked. They heard footsteps inside and then the door snapped open.

"What is it *now*?" shouted a voice. And there

was Patrice, small and plump as ever, glaring at them. She was wrapped in a checked apron, and her black button eyes sparkled fiercely.

"Some friend!" muttered Bilbert.

Jessie stepped back. "Um . . . Patrice, it's me, Jessie. I'm sorry if—"

"*Jessie!*" Patrice's frown disappeared and her face lit up in a big smile. "Come in, dearie, come in!"

She held the door wide. "I thought you were Giff or one of the others, come to beg some fairy-apple cakes again," she explained. "They've been wearing a path to my door all morning. And if I've told them once, I've told them a thousand times, I haven't *got* any fairy-apple cakes."

She wiped her hands on her apron. "They might be Queen Helena's favorite," she went on, "and she might just have come back from her journey around the Realm, and I might wish with all my heart I *did* have some to give her. But I don't, and that's all there is to it!"

Then she noticed Bilbert. She pointed at him suspiciously. "Who's this gnome? What's he doing here?" she demanded. "Is he with you, Jessie?"

Bilbert threw back his shoulders. "I am not 'this gnome,' madam!" he announced grandly. "I am Bilbert the Brave, sent by Queen Jessica to guard the little princess Jessie on her journey to Hidden Valley."

Patrice narrowed her eyes. "Is that so?" she said. "Well *I* am Patrice, the palace housekeeper, and when you get to that valley of yours, I'll thank you to arrange for a cartload of fairy-apples to be sent to the palace immediately. There are none to be had around here at all. And I need some urgently."

Bilbert bowed. Jessie saw his knees wobble.

"Could we come in and sit down for a minute, please, Patrice?" she asked hurriedly. "He—I mean, *we*, are really tired. And I want to ask your help."

"Of course, dearie," said Patrice. She beamed at Jessie, and shot another unfriendly look at Bilbert. It was obvious that she didn't much like the idea of inviting him in, but she realized she had no choice.

She led the way down the narrow corridor to her tiny kitchen.

CHAPTER FIVE

The Journey Begins

There was a loud knock on the front door. Patrice sighed, got up from the table, and went to answer it. Bilbert took the opportunity to grab three more cookies. He bit into them greedily.

"Don't *crunch*, Bilbert," complained Jessie. "And for goodness' sake, brush your beard. It's got cookie crumbs all through it now, as well as everything else."

Bilbert looked down his nose at her. "I can see you're not used to dealing with brave warriors, little princess," he said. "We don't have time to waste making ourselves look pretty."

"No I *haven't!*" screeched Patrice's voice, from the door. "I haven't made any fairy-apple cakes. Stop asking me, or I'll go mad. Madder than I am now, anyway, which is saying something. But you'd better come in. Jessie's here."

"What? Jessie? Hooray!"

Jessie smiled. She recognized that voice. It was Giff the elf. And by the sound of the clattering steps in the corridor, Maybelle was with him.

Sure enough, Giff and Maybelle were soon crowding into the kitchen. They were surprised to see Bilbert, but they greeted Jessie happily.

"Haven't seen you for a while," Maybelle snorted, tossing her white mane with its shiny red ribbons. "Suppose you came to welcome Queen Helena back, did you?"

"Well, not exactly," said Jessie, glancing at Bilbert. "I came to take Bilbert here to Hidden Valley. He's been in our world for a while and—"

"I see," snickered Maybelle, winking at Bilbert, who scowled at her.

"Stayed out in the moonlight, did you?" Maybelle persisted. "Made the old mistake. *When* will you gnomes learn? There must be hundreds of you out there by now. How long were you stuck?"

"For months, we think," said Jessie. "Bilbert can't remember much."

Giff shivered. "Imagine being turned to stone!" he wailed, staring at Bilbert in fascinated horror.

Bilbert lifted his chin. "It's not so bad," he said. "If you're tough." He folded his arms. "Of course, for an elf, or a little pet horse who goes in for ribbons and such, it would be a real problem. I can see that. But it didn't worry *me*."

Maybelle snickered again. "Oh, of course," she retorted. "It didn't worry you, did it? Not at all. Except that now, just like all the others I've seen, you're as weak as a little baby furrybear. And, like all the others, you can't remember your way home. Other than that, you're fine!"

Bilbert opened his mouth to shout a reply, but Jessie held up her hand. "Don't tease, Maybelle," she pleaded. "Just tell me: how do I get Bilbert home? I was hoping Queen Helena could help us, but Patrice says no one can see her. Now I don't know what to do."

"Leave him here," said Maybelle. "Some of his friends are sure to be turning up soon, with more fairy-apples to sell. He can go home with them."

"No," said Jessie stubbornly. "I've got to take him myself. I promised Granny. She said if we took the secret way I could be home at Blue Moon tomorrow."

"Oh," whimpered Giff. "The secret way. Oh dear, oh dear. I don't think you should try to go to Hidden Valley, Jessie. Especially by the secret way. It's *terribly* hard to find. I've been there but I could *never* lead you to it. Oh dear, oh dear!"

"Stop snivelling, Giff," exclaimed Patrice. "Have a cookie and be quiet. I couldn't find the secret way again myself. But there must be *some-one* around here who can."

Maybelle shook her mane. "There is," she said.

"Who, then?" demanded Bilbert. "Come on, horse, spit it out. *Who* knows the secret way?"

"I do," said Maybelle.

Of course, Maybelle made the most of her chance to punish Bilbert for being rude to her. She didn't

48

agree to take him to Hidden Valley just like that.

"I suppose I could take you." She yawned. "If you asked me very, very nicely."

"I would be grateful if you would guide me, horse," muttered Bilbert sulkily.

Maybelle closed her eyes. "Not good enough," she drawled.

"Say 'please,'" whispered Jessie to Bilbert. "Say, 'please, Maybelle.'"

"Please, Maybelle," growled Bilbert.

Maybelle leaned against the wall and crossed her front hooves. She yawned again, showing all her front teeth.

Bilbert fumed. "Listen, horse —" he began, but Jessie nudged him hard and he stopped. He took a deep breath.

"Maybelle," he said through tight lips, "I would be most grateful if you would guide me to Hidden Valley. Please."

"Say, 'pretty please,'" snickered Maybelle.

"Pretty please," snapped Bilbert.

"'Pretty please with sugar on it, and you're not a little pet horse, clever, brave Maybelle.'"

"Pretty please with sugar on it, and you're not a little pet horse, clever, brave Maybelle!" Bilbert was almost purple in the face with rage by now.

Patrice giggled behind her hand.

Maybelle sighed. "Oh, very well then," she said. "Since you ask me so nicely." She pushed herself away from the wall. "Shall we go?"

"I'd love to go with you, but with Queen Helena back I really don't have time. Still, at least I can pack you a few things to eat and drink," said Patrice.

She began pulling things out of the pantry, tripping over Giff every now and then as he poked his nose into jars and packets. She batted at him irritably. "How long will you be away?" she called.

"If all goes well, we should be back by lunchtime tomorrow," Maybelle answered, very businesslike all of a sudden.

"I'll get you to Brill by the secret way," she told Jessie. "That's the easy part. At Brill we'll have to find a guide to take us to the Gap. That will be trickier."

"Giff can go with you," said Patrice, bustling

50

around the kitchen. "It'll get him out of my hair."

"What?" protested Giff. "But . . . But . . ."

"No buts," said Patrice firmly. "You're going. Don't be scared. It won't be like last time. And just think, Giff. You can bring me back some fairy-apples from Hidden Valley. And then I can make some fairy-apple cakes. You'd like that, wouldn't you?"

"Ye-es," said Giff doubtfully.

"We'll have a good time, Giff." Jessie laughed. She was looking forward to her trip now that Maybelle was in charge.

"You'll have to do exactly as I say," Maybelle warned Giff sternly.

Giff's pointed ears drooped. He covered his face with his hands. "Oh dear," he moaned. "The secret way! Brill! Oh dear, oh dear, oh dear . . ."

Not long afterward, Maybelle, Giff, Jessie and Bilbert were walking along a narrow path that wound away from the palace through a thick forest of trees. Maybelle's lips moved silently, as though she was talking to herself.

Jessie helped Bilbert as much as she could, but he tramped slowly, and stumbled over and over again. When she had helped him up for about the tenth time, she shook her head. This was ridiculous. Bilbert was too weak to go on.

"Maybelle," she called.

The little horse stopped and looked back at her. "Three hundred and four," she said. "Three hundred and four . . . Jessie, I'm trying to keep count! What is it?"

"I don't think Bilbert can go much farther," said Jessie.

"Rubbish!" protested Bilbert, becoming very red in the face. "I am perfectly . . ." He swayed dangerously and Jessie caught him just before he tumbled yet again to the ground.

Maybelle curled her lip disdainfully. "It's not far now, Jessie," she said. "The gnome will just have to cope. Three hundred and four. Three hundred and four."

Bilbert turned to Jessie. "As Queen Jessica said, I am a wounded warrior," he stated, puffing out his chest. "It is only right that a warrior should ride. I will ride the horse."

Giff gasped and clapped his hand to his mouth.

Maybelle bared her teeth. "Understand this, gnome," she hissed. "No one rides me. No one ever has. No one ever will."

Bilbert looked sulky.

"Don't argue," pleaded Jessie. "We have to work out what to *do*!"

"There's no need to do anything," snapped Maybelle. "I tell you, we're very nearly at the short-cut. And before you know it we'll be in Brill." She began moving on, keeping her eyes fixed on the trees to her right. "Three hundred and five, three hundred and six," she muttered to herself.

Giff sniffed.

"Be quiet, Giff," Maybelle ordered. "If I lose count, we'll miss it."

"But I don't *want* to go to Hidden Valley!" Giff complained.

"Well, that makes two of us," shouted Bilbert. "I don't want you to either!"

Giff began to wail. His ears were drooping down around his shoulders by now.

Jessie felt sorry for him. She took his hand.

"I'm *glad* you're coming with us, Giff," she whispered. "Take no notice of Bilbert. He's being grumpy and difficult because he's scared. Granny said so."

Giff snuffled into his spotted handkerchief.

"Three hundred and thirteen!" exclaimed Maybelle. She looked closely at the tree beside her. "Yes, I think this is the one."

To Jessie the tree looked exactly like all the others. It was huge, with a strong brown trunk and branches that spread high and wide into the sky.

"Gather round," said Maybelle, tossing her head bossily.

Jessie and the others clustered around the tree.

"Close your eyes and cross your fingers," Maybelle ordered. "Now, I'm going to count to three. And then everyone—and I mean *everyone*—has to shout 'In.' Have you got that?"

"Of course we have," said Bilbert. "We aren't stupid! Well . . ." He darted a look at Giff. "*I'm* not, anyway."

CHAPTER SIX

The Furrybears of Brill

J essie opened her eyes. She was still facing the great tree. She blinked. The magic hadn't worked. Nothing had happened at all.

"Oh, Maybelle!" she cried. She turned around. Then she stared.

The path was still there. But now a little stream rippled beside it. A group of dark green trees that were quite different from any of the others nearby clustered on the other side of the stream. And behind them rose a steep, rocky mountain.

Someone nudged her arm and she jumped.

"Surprised?" Maybelle asked, crossing her

front legs and looking very pleased with herself.

Jessie gulped and nodded. "I thought we hadn't gone anywhere," she said. "This tree looks just like the other one."

"They all look alike," Maybelle said smugly. She looked at the sky and then nodded at Bilbert and Giff, who were standing by the edge of the stream. "Let's collect those two and get going," she said. "I think it's going to rain. And it's getting late."

Jessie's eyes widened in surprise. But then she looked up at the cloudy sky and saw that Maybelle was right. When they had started out it was early morning, but now the sun was high. Somehow or other, hours had passed.

Giff came running over to her and tugged at her arm. "Jessie," he said fearfully. "Something's wrong with Bilbert!"

Jessie ran to see, and found Bilbert standing absolutely still, staring at the running stream. He licked his lips and shook his head. His eyes were fixed and glassy.

Jessie bent down to him. "Bilbert! Bilbert!" she called. "What on earth's wrong?"

Bilbert didn't reply.

"Don't worry about him." Maybelle sniffed, coming over to them and nudging Bilbert with one hoof. "He's probably getting his memory back."

Jessie saw Bilbert's eyelids flutter. Slowly he turned his eyes toward Maybelle.

"The gnomes who come back from your world always go strange when their memories start to come back," Maybelle continued. "I've seen it before, over and over again. And the closer they get to home, the stranger they go. Silly things!"

"Watch your mouth, horse!" grunted Bilbert. With a great effort, he straightened his shoulders and turned away from the trees.

"Did you remember something, Bilbert?" asked Jessie, before he and Maybelle could start arguing again.

He nodded. "Just a flash," he said. "Very clear. I remember being here. Standing right here, looking at the stream. And . . ." He paused.

"Go on!" begged Jessie.

"And I was worried," said Bilbert. "I was very worried about something. But I was excited too.

Because . . ." He frowned, thinking hard.

". . . Because of something I'd just heard," he went on slowly. "Someone had just told me something that was going to solve the problem."

"What problem?" demanded Maybelle.

Bilbert shook his head. "I don't know," he said in bewilderment.

"What did you hear?" squeaked Giff.

"I don't know that either," growled Bilbert.

"Well, who told you?" urged Jessie.

Bilbert looked at her in surprise. "One of the furrybears, I suppose. Who else would it be, around here? No one else to talk to."

"*Furrybears?*"

"Oh, yes." Maybelle sighed. "I haven't told you about them, have I?"

She jerked her head at the strange trees on the other side of the stream. "They're in there. They'll be watching us now. Getting their traps ready, probably. Come on. No point in standing here."

She began walking toward a little bridge that crossed the stream. Giff followed. He'd started whimpering again.

"Traps?" exclaimed Jessie, hurrying after them with Bilbert.

"Yes!" Maybelle snapped. "Jessie, why do you keep repeating everything we say?"

"Well . . ." Jessie swallowed. "Well, because I don't know what you're talking about, Maybelle. I've never heard of furrybears. And why would they want to trap us?"

"So we'll tell them a story," sniveled Giff. "Oh dear, oh dear!"

"A *story?*"

Maybelle rolled her eyes. "Oh, please, don't start that again." She sighed. "Listen, Jessie; it's simple. The furrybears love stories. Right? They collect them from anyone who comes this way."

"And that's not many," Bilbert put in. "Most of the time, the furrybears live here on their own. Telling stories."

"*Telling*—" Jessie began. She saw Maybelle glaring at her and stopped herself just in time.

"Telling stories," Bilbert said again. "They just sit around up in the trees, eating leaves and honey cakes, making traps to drop on any stranger who

61

might come along, and telling the same old stories to each other over and over again. What an awful life!"

"It doesn't sound so bad," said Jessie. "Not everyone wants to dig for gold all day. I like stories myself."

"They trapped Patrice and me when we were here," wailed Giff. "In a big net that they threw from the trees. And we had to tell them *six* stories before they'd let us go. Stories they hadn't heard before too. It was *awful*! I couldn't think of *anything*."

"Naturally," drawled Maybelle.

"Poor Giff," murmured Jessie, trying not to smile.

Giff sniffed. "In the end, Patrice did it. She told them stories about the palace. Things she knew but no one else did. Like what happened when your grandmother ran away to your world, Jessie. And what happened when the trolls tried to take over the Realm, and how the griffins saved the flower fairies from the giant spiders. And—"

"Shh!" warned Maybelle.

Jessie froze. They had crossed the stream now, and there was a rustling and tittering coming from the trees ahead.

"Now leave this to me," the little horse ordered.

She trotted forward and stopped a safe distance away from any overhanging branches. She bowed.

"Furrybears of Brill," she shouted. "I am Maybelle, the leader of this party. I have been here before. Pay attention to me!"

The rustling and tittering stopped.

"She saw us!" squeaked a small, disappointed voice from the nearest tree.

"I know your tricks," shouted Maybelle sternly. "And I tell you now, furrybears of Brill, that our mission is very important and cannot wait. We must go to Hidden Valley. We have no time now to tell you a tale."

There was silence from the trees.

Maybelle shook her mane. "You will *not* try to trap us today," she said firmly. "Instead, you will choose one among you to be our guide to the Gap. And when we return —"

"Come a bit closer," squeaked a sly little voice. "We can't hear you."

Maybelle stood where she was. "None of your nonsense!" she said. "I tell you, you will *not* try to trap us today."

Again there was silence. Maybelle thought for a moment. Then she looked up.

"If you do as I say," she said slowly and clearly, "you will be rewarded." She nudged Jessie forward so that she stood in clear view.

"This human child is Jessie, the granddaughter of Jessica, our true Queen," Maybelle went on. "I'm sure you've already heard the story of Jessie, and how, once upon a time, she saved the Realm from the Queen's wicked cousin Valda."

There were sharp squeaks of interest from the leaves. Jessie looked carefully into the dark mass of green, but she could see nothing. The furry-bears were very well hidden.

Maybelle took a deep breath. "If you will help us on our way now, we will return to Brill tomorrow, and . . ." She paused dramatically. "Princess Jessie will then tell you the best story ever told

CHAPTER SEVEN

The Thorns

The little creature's fur was fluffy and brown. It had a small black nose and shiny dark eyes. It clasped its soft paws in front of its round stomach and bowed. It was so cute and cuddly-looking that Jessie's arms ached to pick it up. She began to reach out.

"Don't do it," warned Maybelle out of the corner of her mouth. "Once they get on your knee or in your arms you're stuck with them."

Jessie pulled her arms back and clamped them firmly to her sides.

The furrybear fixed its twinkling eyes on her.

It puffed its little chest and spoke.

"Greetings, Princess Jessie, I am Fubsy 44," it squeaked.

Jessie blinked.

"They have to use numbers because they're all called Fubsy," explained Maybelle. "Every one of them. Don't ask me why."

The furrybear heard her and put its head on one side. "Fubsy's a nice name, isn't it?" it asked anxiously.

"Oh yes," Jessie assured it. "Lovely."

Fubsy 44 looked pleased. "Thank you," it said. "Now. Your story, Princess Jessie. Will it really be the best story we've ever heard?"

Jessie swallowed and nodded.

"Will the story begin with 'once upon a time' and end 'so they lived happily ever after?'" asked Fubsy 44.

"Yes," said Jessie. "Yes, I can promise that."

"Then we agree!" Fubsy 44 squealed.

The trees suddenly came back to life. Dozens of silken ropes flew from the branches. Dozens of furrybears began to slide down them and bounce to the leafy ground.

They clustered, chattering, around Jessie, touching her clothes with their small paws and looking up at her with wondering eyes. They all looked exactly alike. And they all talked at once.

"Could we go now?" muttered Bilbert, edging away. "These midget fluff-balls make me nervous."

"You're Bilbert," piped up Fubsy 44. Its nose twitched. "You told the story of the waterfall sprites and the snairies. It was very short."

Bilbert shrugged. Then his eyes narrowed. "You remember me?" he demanded. "When was I here?"

"Six months ago," squeaked Fubsy 44, staring. "You were going down the path. To the palace."

"Yes, yes," chattered all the other furrybears. "Bilbert of Hidden Valley. The snairies and the waterfall sprites. Once upon a time—"

Jessie held up her hand. "Just a minute," she called through the noise, as the whole crowd began chanting Bilbert's story.

The furrybears stopped talking immediately. "Are you going to tell us a story now?" said one of the smallest, hopefully.

"No," said Jessie. "Tomorrow. After I've been to Hidden Valley. Right now I want you to tell me something. I want to—test your memories. What happened when Bilbert came here before?"

Fubsy 44 spread its paws. "The gnome Bilbert came," it said. "We trapped him with a—net and twig trap, I think."

The other furrybears nodded vigorously. "Net and twig," they agreed.

Bilbert scowled at them.

"He told us the story of the snairies and the waterfall sprites," Fubsy 44 repeated. Its face brightened. "Once upon a time—" it began.

"No, *no*!" Jessie laughed in spite of herself. "No stories. Stories tomorrow. What happened with Bilbert then?"

"Then we told *him* stories," said Fubsy 44. "Lots and lots. We gave him some honey cakes. We looked after him all night long. But he wasn't glad."

Bilbert groaned. "I'll bet I wasn't glad," he said. "But I am now. I'm glad I can't remember."

Fubsy 44 looked down at its small feet. "We

told him all our best ones too," it whispered.

"I'm sure you did," said Jessie. Her hands tingled with the urge to pick up the little creature and comfort it, but she remembered Maybelle's warning and folded her arms tightly in front of her instead.

"Which one of you will take us to the Gap that leads to Hidden Valley?" asked Maybelle.

"I will," said Fubsy 44, still looking at its feet.

"Thank you," said Maybelle. She shook her mane. "Shall we go, then?"

With the furrybears chattering around them, the friends walked into the shade of the dark green trees. A thick carpet of leaves cushioned the ground under their feet.

Once her eyes got used to the dimness, Jessie could see, high above her head, a tangle of branches, built all over with little houses, platforms, walkways, ladders and slides. A whole village in the trees. Dozens of ropes dangled from the branches, and everywhere were nets, boxes and cages of twigs waiting to be dropped on unsuspecting visitors.

Soon they reached the place where the trees ended. Jessie stepped out of the shade. The sun had disappeared behind a veil of gray clouds. She looked in dismay at what was in front of her. She was standing on a narrow strip of grass dotted with yellow flowers. But not far ahead, a thick tangle of thorny bushes rose high, spreading out on both sides for as far as she could see.

It reminded her of the blackberry thicket that grew at the end of the Wyldwood garden, blocking off the fence to Blue Moon, but it was a hundred times bigger. Behind it was a mountain — a steep wall of jagged, wicked-looking rock.

Jessie glanced around at her little group. A miniature horse, a scared elf, a limping gnome and a tiny furrybear. How could they ever get through those thorns? How could they ever climb that mountain?

As far as she could see, it was quite impossible.

Bilbert had stopped and was staring straight ahead with the glassy look Jessie had seen before. Only she noticed it. Maybelle and Giff were too busy trying to hurry Fubsy 44. It had decided that it had to hug every one of its friends before they could leave.

"Bilbert," Jessie whispered to him. "Are you remembering something?"

"The fairy-apple trees," he droned. "Trouble." His face crumpled. "Oh, what have we done?"

"Something's wrong with the fairy-apple trees?" asked Jessie, shaking his arm gently. "What is it?"

"Pick the apples from dawn to dark," muttered Bilbert, still staring strangely. "Leave nothing on the trees to fall and spoil. Every fairy-apple is another coin for our store. Every year we pick harder and faster. But . . . but . . ." He covered his grubby face with his hands and swayed.

"Bilbert!" cried Jessie in fright.

Maybelle looked up from the furrybears' farewell and came trotting over to them, with Giff close behind. She looked closely at the swaying gnome and nudged him with her nose.

"Wake up," she said. "Wake up, gnome. You'll soon be home."

Bilbert blinked. He licked his dry lips. "Have to

hurry," he said. "We have to hurry."

"All right then," shouted Maybelle. "Come on!"

She glanced back at the furrybears. Fubsy 44 had finally finished hugging, but was obviously tempted to start all over again. It was still standing by the trees, looking longingly at its friends.

"Don't forget. The best story in the history of Brill!" Maybelle called sharply. "But only if we leave now!"

Fubsy 44 lowered its head and, giving its friends a final wave, began to toddle across the grass toward them.

"Really," scoffed Maybelle. "You'd think it was going to be away for a month instead of an hour." She turned to Bilbert. "Now, pull yourself together, gnome. Next stop, Hidden Valley."

But Maybelle was wrong. There were many, many stops over the next few hours.

Jessie soon found out why they needed their furrybear guide. The tangle of prickly bushes really was a hundred times thicker and higher than the hedge of blackberries that grew between Blue

Moon and Wyldwood. But it was possible to go through it—if you knew the way—because it was threaded with dozens of tunnels.

The tunnels twisted and turned, running into each other and off to the sides. It was like a maze. A maze you had to crawl through, if you were as tall as Jessie.

Fubsy 44 went first, followed by Bilbert. Then came Jessie, Giff and Maybelle. Bilbert was very weak. He kept falling and having to rest. And every time he did, Fubsy 44 became more nervous and impatient.

Jessie crawled along blindly, feeling thorns snagging her hair and her clothes. If we take the wrong turn, we could be lost in here forever, she thought. If Fubsy 44 decides it's tired of all this stopping and starting, or starts to miss its friends too much, it might just run back home and leave us. Then we'll never get out. This wasn't a nice thought, and she tried to put it out of her mind.

Ahead of her, Bilbert groaned and crumpled to the ground yet again. Fubsy 44 stopped and looked back at him with bright, questioning eyes.

"How far to the Gap?" called Maybelle.

"Not long," squeaked Fubsy 44. Its furry ears twitched. "Let's go."

"Bilbert has to rest," Jessie said.

Fubsy 44 blinked at her. "I want to go home now," it said. It started to edge away.

"No!" begged Jessie. "Please, no."

The little creature took no notice.

Jessie racked her brains. She had to stop the furrybear from leaving. But how? How could she convince it to stay?

Then she had an inspiration. There was something no furrybear could resist.

"Fubsy 44," she called. "Fubsy 44! Please, tell us a story!"

CHAPTER EIGHT

Hidden Valley

Fubsy 44 beamed, scuttled back to Jessie's side, and plumped itself on the ground. "Once upon a time," it began in a soft, singsong voice, "there was a beautiful princess called Jessica. She fell in love with a man called Robert, who loved her as much as she loved him . . ."

"Oh no," complained Giff, from behind. "That's the story Patrice told the furrybears years ago, when they trapped us. Couldn't we have something new?"

"Shh," hissed Jessie, as the furrybear's voice droned on. She didn't care what the story was.

The important thing was to keep Fubsy 44 busy while Bilbert rested.

". . . So kind Patrice gave Robert two fairy-apples," Fubsy 44 was saying. "And she said to him, 'Take these to eat on your journey, and plant the seeds in your world. Then more fairy-apple trees will grow, to remind my darling Jessica of home.' And Robert promised."

Giff sniffed. Jessie looked around and saw that tears were running down his cheeks. "That bit always makes me cry," he explained. Behind him, Maybelle snorted in disgust.

Jessie turned back to check on Bilbert. His eyelids were flickering. He seemed to be listening to the story. Soon he would be ready to start moving again.

And just in time too. Because Fubsy 44 was finishing. ". . . And so Queen Helena ruled in her sister Jessica's place," it said. "And at the house called Blue Moon, Robert, Jessica and the fairy-apple trees lived happily ever after." It sat back and sighed with contentment.

"That's what you said before. You told me that

story when I was in Brill!" cried Bilbert suddenly. He scrambled to his feet. "I remember now!" His beard was wildly tangled, his dirty clothes were almost in rags, torn by the thorns. He shook his fist in the air.

"I thought our problem was solved," he shouted. "I went through the Door, into the human world. I searched and searched. But I could only find one fairy-apple tree. It was old and small and weak, with hardly any apples on it."

Fubsy 44 stared at him in fright. "I think I'll go home now," it said.

Jessie grabbed Bilbert by the arm to quiet him. "No, Fubsy 44," she said calmly and sternly. "You'll take us on to the Gap, as you promised. Or I won't tell you and your friends the best story in the history of Brill."

"We mean it!" Maybelle shouted.

Fubsy 44 ducked its head and obediently began to trot in front of them once more.

Thunder rumbled overhead. Bilbert stumbled forward bravely. Jessie crawled after him, terrified that he'd fall again. And wondering. So Bilbert hadn't found the Wyldwood fairy-apple tree just by chance. He'd gone looking for it, because of the story the furrybears had told him.

But why? Surely he wasn't so keen on money that he'd travel all the way to the human world, and face all those dangers, just to collect a few more fairy-apples to sell?

Ahead, Fubsy 44 squeaked with joy. Bilbert began moving faster.

Jessie saw dim light shining at the end of the thorny tunnel and sighed with relief. At last they had arrived at the Gap. Whatever the Gap was.

The rock towered high above them. Jessie looked around as Giff and Maybelle came out of the thorny tunnel behind her. "Where's this Gap?" she asked.

Maybelle ambled over to a patch of tall, spiky grass. "Here," she said. She brushed the grass aside and Jessie saw a long, narrow opening in the rock.

"We go through here," Maybelle said. "It's a tight squeeze, but I've done it before. Hidden Valley's only a few minutes away now. Through the

Gap, and down the hill. We'll be in the village by sunset. With luck, before we get wet. By the sound of that thunder, the rain can't be far away."

She looked sideways at Bilbert. "He'd better have another rest before we go on, though." She sniffed. "He'll get all his memory back as soon as he goes through the Gap. It'll weaken him for a while. We don't want him fainting on us. Why don't we eat?"

"I go now!" squeaked Fubsy 44. It darted away into the thorn bushes without waiting for an answer.

"How are we going to get back through the thorns without Fubsy 44?" asked Jessie nervously. She hadn't thought about this before.

"One of the gnomes will take us," Maybelle answered. "We only needed the furrybear because Bilbert can't remember at the moment."

They sat down to eat, leaning against the rock. Patrice had packed soft rolls and cheese, a bag full of purple fruits that Jessie had never seen before, and some chewy, nutty cakes. There was a pink drink too, in a silver bottle. It was deliciously cool on Jessie's dry throat and she sipped at it grate-fully.

Bilbert took his share of food and began to eat it greedily, as usual. Soon his clothes, face and beard were covered with purple juice stains and fresh crumbs.

"Your beard really is disgusting," frowned Maybelle. "It's all full of seeds and crumbs. Why didn't you wash it in the river while you had the chance?"

"Waste of time," Bilbert mumbled.

Maybelle turned her back on him and watched Giff packing up the remains of the food. "You're a good elf," she said to him. "Good and *clean*."

Bilbert was looking better after his meal, Jessie thought. Messier, but better.

He stood up. "Let's go," he said. "I want to get back to the valley. It drives me crazy not to be able to remember things." He strode to the Gap and began to push through it.

"Come on," said Jessie to the others.

One by one they followed the gnome through the narrow gap in the rock.

They had been walking for only a few minutes when they heard Bilbert's cry. "No!" he was shouting in desperation. "No! No! No!"

Jessie rushed forward. And then, quite suddenly, she had reached him, and was looking down into Hidden Valley.

Her first feeling was bitter disappointment. "The most beautiful place in all the Realm," Granny had said. But Hidden Valley wasn't beautiful at all. Just flat, bare, sunbaked earth surrounded by rocky mountains, with a sad-looking little village sitting in the middle.

"How could this place have been one of Granny's favorites?" she said to Maybelle. "And where are these famous fairy-apple trees?"

Behind her, Maybelle gasped with shock. And it was only then that Jessie realized exactly what she had said.

Where *were* the fairy-apple trees?

They should be blossoming now. Hundreds of them. She should be looking down on a sea of palest pink. The air should be filled with the scent of blossom.

But there was nothing. Just houses, a bit of tired grass, and a few low bushes dotted about.

"Bilbert!" whispered Maybelle. "The *trees*. What's *happened*?"

Bilbert had crumpled to the ground. "Gone," he groaned. "All gone."

"But . . ." Maybelle shook her head. "That's impossible."

Bilbert stared at the ugly valley below. "Fairy-apple trees don't live long," he said. "They grow fast, and they die fast."

Maybelle snorted. "But as fast as the old trees die, new ones grow to take their places. It happens in a moment. I've seen it myself."

But Jessie was looking into Bilbert's hopeless eyes. She was remembering things he had said: *Pick the apples from dawn to dark . . . Leave nothing on the trees to fall and spoil . . . Every fairy-apple is another coin for our store . . . Every year we pick harder and faster . . .*

Suddenly she knew what had happened to the fairy-apple trees. Her throat ached with sadness.

Bilbert slumped miserably on the ground, his

head bent low. At last he had his wish. He remembered. Everything. And he wasn't boasting Bilbert the Brave anymore.

"What's happened?" whispered Giff.

"Last season, for the first time, the gnomes actually did what they'd been trying to do for years," said Jessie, looking down at the dry, flat valley. "They managed to pick every single fairy-apple on their trees. They worked so hard. They didn't leave one. They didn't even eat any themselves. They wanted the money the apples would bring at the market."

Bilbert moaned. Tears were rolling down his cheeks.

"At the end of the picking there were no spoilt apples on the ground," Jessie went on softly. "The gnomes were very pleased with themselves. But they'd forgotten something."

Overhead the thunder growled. The sky was very dark.

"After the apples went to market we started pulling down the old, dying trees for our bonfires, as we always did," wept Bilbert. "But when they were gone, no new trees grew. At first we didn't understand it. We kept waiting and waiting for the new shoots to come. But none did."

He paused, while the others looked down at the sad, empty land below.

"Then we realized what we'd done," he said. "We'd done what we set out to do. We'd sold every fairy-apple in the valley. Our storehouse was full of gold. But there were no rotten apples or cores on the ground. So there were no seeds. No seeds at all."

jessie saves the Day

"How could you have been so stupid!" exclaimed Maybelle.

Bilbert shook his head. "We . . . only thought about the money," he whispered, and put his face in his hands.

Maybelle's white tail lashed. "This . . . this is *awful*!" she cried. "And no one outside has any idea of it."

"We knew we had to keep what we'd done a secret," said Bilbert. "Otherwise the whole Realm would know how stupid we'd been. Already they laugh at us, for loving gold."

He sighed. "I . . . I said I'd go to Queen Helena and ask for some fairy-apples from the storehouse, to plant. We knew she'd be angry with us. But at least she'd keep our secret. And we had no choice."

"Then on the way, in Brill, you heard a story that made you think my grandmother had some fairy-apple trees at Blue Moon," said Jessie. "And you went there instead."

Bilbert nodded. "That way, I thought no one would ever know what the gnomes of Hidden Valley had done. I thought it would be a great adventure too. I thought I'd be a great hero. But instead . . ."

Tears started rolling down his cheeks again. "Instead, I was a fool. I found the tree. I ate six apples, all in a row, and then I started fishing. I fell asleep. And when I woke up . . . you were there, and Queen Jessica. It was six months later, and my memory, and the fairy-apples, were gone. All gone."

There was a terrible silence. Heavy drops of rain began to fall from the gray sky.

"Come down to the village," said Jessie quietly. "We'll find your friends."

Bilbert staggered to his feet. He took a step and

stumbled. "I can't," he groaned. "I can't face them. What will they say to me? I failed them. I failed my village. I failed the Realm. Because of me Hidden Valley has lost its beauty. And there'll be no more fairy-apples. Ever."

Giff tugged at Jessie's sleeve. "But he can go and get fairy-apples from your tree next season, can't he?"

Jessie bit her lip. "No," she said. "The tree is dead. Bilbert knows that."

"The last fairy-apple tree?" quavered Giff.

Bilbert swayed. The rain beat down on his bowed head.

Maybelle stepped forward. "Come on," she said gently. "Get on my back."

Giff watched, his mouth open in astonishment, as Jessie helped Bilbert up onto the slim white back that had never felt a rider. And, her heart full of pity, Maybelle broke her golden rule and carried Bilbert the Brave home.

They stopped just outside the village. No light showed in the windows of any of the houses. There was no beauty or life anywhere. The rain splashed down on flat, brown earth. Here and there a small gray heap of wet ashes lay. The gnomes had been burning thorn bushes. They had no tree wood to make cheery bonfires now.

"Where *is* everyone?" asked Jessie.

Bilbert slid from Maybelle's back. "They must still be in the mines," he said. He turned his sad gaze back to the ugly ground, the limp tufts of grass, the cold little houses in the village. "You can see why they wouldn't be hurrying home."

As he spoke, Giff pricked up his ears. "I can hear them," he said. "They're coming."

Jessie listened carefully. Gradually she too began to hear the sound of many shuffling feet in the distance.

"I can't bear it!" groaned Bilbert. "Oh, what will they say to me? What will I do? They've waited so long. They depended on me. And I've come back empty-handed." He kicked at the dirt.

"Once this was a forest of fairy-apple trees," he said. "And Hidden Valley was the most beautiful place in the Realm." He put his hand out to

Maybelle. "Wasn't it?" he pleaded. "*Wasn't it?*"

"Yes, it was," said Maybelle.

Giff started to sob.

"All gone now," moaned Bilbert. "All gone."

He stood before them, his shoulders bowed. His clothes were ragged and filthy. His face was streaked with mud, rain and tears. His hair and beard were a mess. You could hardly see their proper color anymore.

The sound of approaching footsteps grew louder. The villagers were on their way.

Jessie felt helpless and unhappy. She hated seeing proud Bilbert like this—so sad and lost-looking. She remembered him sitting at the kitchen table at Blue Moon talking grandly about Bilbert the Brave. She remembered how surprised and disgusted she'd been as she watched him stuffing himself with toast, spraying crumbs all around.

She almost smiled at the memory. Granny hadn't been surprised at all. Neither had Patrice, when he ate in her kitchen. Hidden Valley gnomes must be famous for their messy eating habits. Maybe that's why the men all had beards, to catch the things that fell from their mouths.

Jessie jumped. She remembered how Bilbert had looked when she first met him. She remembered him crunching pears at Blue Moon. Her thoughts raced. Was it possible . . . ? Could it be . . . ?

"Bilbert!" she shrieked. "Bilbert, brush your beard!"

"Jessie, don't bother him about that now!" rumbled Maybelle, nudging her.

"Just do as I say, Bilbert. Brush it!" Jessie insisted. "Comb it through with your fingers. Now! Quick!"

Bilbert stared at her. And then he raised trembling hands to his beard and slowly began combing his fingers through the messy hair.

Twigs, leaves and crumbs scattered onto the rain-soaked, muddy ground. Twigs, leaves, crumbs, bits of spiderweb, flower petals—and seeds.

"Seeds!" Jessie yelled. "You've got seeds in your beard. A lot of them were there when I first saw you. I think they're the seeds from the fairy-apples you ate at Wyldwood. And the ones that fell on you later. They might, they might—"

With a scream, Giff pointed.

There, in the wet earth at Bilbert's feet, was a tiny green shoot. Bilbert stared at it as if he couldn't believe his eyes. He took a step back.

Giff screamed again, pointed again. And there were two more shoots, growing taller as they watched.

"*Jessie!*" shouted Maybelle. "Jessie, you've done it, you've done it! Fairy-apple trees! Fairy-apple trees!"

"More!" squealed Jessie, dancing with delight. "More, Bilbert, more!"

Bilbert didn't have to be asked again. He began rubbing his beard so hard and so fast that it fluffed out and flew around his shoulders. And as he did, more seeds scattered and fell to the wet and muddy ground. More shoots appeared. And they grew, and grew.

By the time the villagers heard their shouting and started running, the trees were as tall as Jessie's shoulder. By the time Bilbert's friends, running faster than any of the others, had reached his side, fairy-apple branches were waving over Jessie's head.

By the time the rain had stopped and the clouds had rolled away, the setting sun was shining not on a bare patch of earth, but on a small sea of whispering pale-pink blossom.

Roaring, cheering, singing, laughing, crying with happiness and relief, the gnomes of Hidden Valley surrounded Bilbert, Jessie, Maybelle and Giff, shaking their hands, clapping them on the back. Their long, sad wait was over. Their beautiful valley, so nearly destroyed forever, was saved.

The celebrations went on for hours. Jessie finally fell asleep at midnight. And all night long her dreams were filled with the whispering, rustling sound of the fairy-apple trees that had come home.

The next morning, Maybelle, Giff, Jessie and Bilbert met in the village square. Dozens of gnomes chatted and bustled around them, and gnome children rushed about with wooden toys of all kinds. A holiday had been declared in Hidden Valley. There would be no work for anyone today.

"I wish you could stay longer," Bilbert said. In fresh, clean clothes, with pink cheeks and a freshly brushed beard, he looked and sounded like a different gnome.

"I'd like to stay," said Jessie honestly. "But I want to go home too. Do you know what I mean?"

"Oh yes," said Bilbert. He looked around the square, at his friends, and away to where the fairy-apple trees stretched their branches in the sun. "I know just what you mean."

He shuffled his feet in an embarrassed sort of way, then held out a small box. "Don't open it until you get home," he muttered.

Jessie took the box. It was heavier than it looked. "Oh, Bilbert," she cried. "I don't want — "

"A reward," Bilbert finished for her. "I know. But this isn't a reward, little princess. It's a thank-you present. For you and Queen Jessica, from me. And don't worry. It's not gold." He grinned. "It's something much, much better."

CHAPTER TEN

Happy Endings

J essie wanted to go home, all right, but she wasn't looking forward to the journey there. The long crawl through the thorn bush maze would be the worst part. But ever since she'd woken up, she'd also been thinking about the furrybears and the story she had to tell them.

The best story ever told in the history of Brill? How on earth could she manage that?

Suddenly there was an excited shout from outside the village. Everyone in the square stopped, and looked, and ran toward the sound.

Jessie and the others ran after them. They found

the gnomes near the fairy-apple trees, looking up, pointing, and chattering in surprise.

There in the pale blue sky was what looked like a cloud of butterflies.

"Queen Helena!" squeaked Giff in delight.

"The Queen was here only yesterday," exclaimed Bilbert. "My brothers told me so. She came as part of her journey around the Realm. She found out about the fairy-apple trees."

"The Queen was very sad when she saw the trees were gone," piped up a gnome child standing near them. "She cried, the Queen did."

"That's probably why she wasn't seeing anyone when we visited the palace," said Jessie. "She was probably trying to think of what she could do about the fairy-apple trees."

Bilbert puffed out his chest. "Well, I solved that problem for her, didn't I?" he boasted.

Maybelle snorted.

Bilbert rubbed his nose. "Well—*we* solved the problem," he said.

The butterfly cloud was nearer now, and Jessie could see that it was actually hundreds of laughing, winged fairies pulling a floating boat of gold, thin as an eggshell. Inside the boat sat Queen Helena, her long red hair blowing behind her in the wind. She was looking down, waving and smiling. She had seen them. And she had seen the fairy-apple trees.

Slowly the boat came nearer and then, one by one as the fairies dropped the ribbons with which they were pulling it, it began to drift to the ground.

The gnomes crowded around. "Bilbert did it!" they called out to their Queen, pointing at the fairy-apple trees. "Bilbert and Jessie did it!"

"And Maybelle and Giff," added Bilbert, grinning.

Queen Helena stepped out of the boat and took Jessie's hand. "Patrice told me you were here," she said. "I came to find you. But I didn't expect—all this." She gazed in delight at the blooming fairy-apple trees. "I might have known you would work magic for us again, Jessie." She smiled.

Jessie blushed. "Oh, it wasn't *magic*," she said. "It was just—"

"Human common sense," cried Queen Helena, Maybelle and Giff together. And they laughed.

After that there was a rush of excitement, and chatter, and good-byes. And soon Jessie, Giff and Maybelle were sitting with Helena in the golden boat, sailing high over the rocky hill. They were going to stop at Brill. In spite of Maybelle's protests, Jessie didn't want to break her promise to the furrybears.

But as the boat sank gently to the ground, she realized with a sinking heart that she still hadn't thought of a tale to tell them. And they were coming—sliding down from the trees, running as fast as their short little legs would carry them.

"When we've finished here," whispered Queen Helena, as they waited for the crowd to surround them, "you must tell me everything, *everything* that has happened, Jessie. The whole wonderful story."

Jessie looked at her, blinked and sighed with relief.

"Thank you, Your Majesty," she said.

Helena looked bewildered. "Why are you

thanking me?" she asked.

Jessie smiled. "Wait and see," she said.

"A story! A story!" shouted the furrybears, clustering around them. "You promised! The best story ever told in Brill."

"All right," said Jessie, sitting on the edge of the golden boat. "Are you ready?"

"Yes!" chorused the furrybears.

"Especially me!" piped up Fubsy 44, and climbed on her knee.

Jessie laughed. And then she began.

"Once upon a time," she said, "in a house called Blue Moon, a human girl named Jessie found her grandmother looking at a painting. 'The fairy-apple trees . . .' her grandmother murmured, and the charm bracelet on her wrist jingled softly as she raised her hand to touch the painting in front of her . . ."

Jessie's voice went on, soft in the sweet morning air. The furrybears listened, eyes fixed on her face. Queen Helena listened, eyes filled with wonder. And Maybelle and Giff listened too, because although they knew the end of the story, they didn't know the beginning.

At last Jessie came to the end of her story.

"And so . . ." she said, "Jessie came back to Brill and told the story of her adventures to the furrybears. And after that she went home to Blue Moon and her family. And she, and Bilbert, and the gnomes of Hidden Valley, and Patrice and Giff and Maybelle . . ."

"And the furrybears!" squeaked Fubsy 44.

"And Queen Helena!" shrilled another furrybear.

Jessie nodded. "And the furrybears, and Queen Helena, and the fairy-apple trees—and everyone else—lived happily ever after."

"The end," breathed Fubsy 44.

All the furrybears started to clap and cheer.

Fubsy 44 patted Jessie's hand. "That really was the best story we ever heard," he whispered. "You know why?"

Jessie shook her head.

"Because *we* were in it!" squeaked Fubsy 44.

"Yes," Jessie agreed. "That's always the best sort of story. As long as it's got a happy ending."

Much, much later, Jessie was sitting with her grandmother in the Blue Moon kitchen. She'd had a long, hot bath. She'd changed her clothes. She'd eaten two sandwiches and a huge slice of chocolate cake, and drunk a glass of lemon drink with ice in it. She was very tired, very full, and very happy.

"Well." Rosemary smiled as she came through the door. "You two look as if you've had a wonderful time while I've been gone."

She dropped her car keys on the table, bent to kiss Jessie, and turned to Granny. "Oh, by the way, Mum," she said, "I met Mr. Bins outside. He told me to tell you that the little tree you call the fairy-apple—the one in the Wyldwood garden—had died. He seemed rather pleased. What an awful man he is."

"Quite awful," said Granny placidly. "But one day Mr. Bins will get what he deserves. People like him usually do, I find. In the meantime, I don't mind so much about the poor little fairy-apple tree. It was very, very old. It's quite extraordinary that it lived so long, really. Maybe it was waiting—

till it was needed."

Rosemary shook her head. "Mum," she said, "you say the most extraordinary things sometimes."

Granny smiled. "Anyway, Rosemary," she said, "we have a fairy-apple tree of our own now, thanks to Jessie."

She pointed to the little plant standing proudly in its pot at the end of the table.

Rosemary looked at her curiously. "Jessie? Did she find that seedling for you?"

Granny put her head on one side. "It was a thank-you present," she said honestly. "A fairy-apple seedling, in its own home soil! A gift more precious than gold."

"It's very small," Rosemary said doubtfully. "Don't be disappointed if it doesn't grow, Mum."

"Oh, it'll grow!" Granny laughed. "We're going to plant it later, down by the secret garden. Once it can spread out its roots, it'll grow like mad. You just watch it."

Jessie laughed and touched the tiny fairy-apple tree with a gentle finger. Its leaves quivered. She knew it was longing to escape from its pot and reach for the sun.

"And you've got a new charm, Jessie," exclaimed her mother, noticing her bracelet. "A little leaf—just like the leaves on the fairy-apple tree."

She turned to Granny. "Mum, you do spoil her," she scolded.

Granny smiled and said nothing.

Jessie remembered how Queen Helena had kissed her cheek as she pressed the tiny package into her hand just before Jessie disappeared through the Door.

"Thank you, Jessie," she had whispered. "Come back to see us very soon. Don't forget."

Rosemary looked carefully at the bracelet. "The charms are pretty," she said.

"And every one tells a story," Granny said. She winked at Jessie. "I wonder how many more there are to come?"

"Lots, I hope," Jessie said. She sat back in her chair and beamed at them both. "And every one with a happy ending."

Turn the page for a peek at
Jessie's next adventure in the

BOOK 5

The Magic Key

S tuck on the door was a scribbled note: GON FOR HUNNEY. BAK SOON. KUM IN. KEY UNDER MAT.

"What's happened?" whispered Jessie. But, really, she knew the answer.

The golden key was magic. When she'd picked it up, it had made her shrink — to pixie size.

The toadstool was a pixie house, like the toadstools in her grandfather's paintings. And the key she was holding was the key to the door. The pixie who lived in the house must have left it there, expecting friends to call in.

Jessie looked over her shoulder. She could see nothing stirring in the pine glade.

"I'll just have a quick look inside," she said to herself.

She put the key in the lock and turned it. The door swung open to reveal the cutest little room Jessie had ever seen.

Its rounded white walls seemed to glow with soft light. There was a rug of bright green moss on the floor. A hammock made from spiderweb hung in one corner. That must be where the pixie sleeps, Jessie thought.

The room was very tidy. All around the walls hung bunches of red and orange berries, like balloons.

In the middle of the room was a round table covered with bright red mats. On the mats were several brown bowls piled high with cakes, cookies, and round purple-blue fruits that looked like big plums. Right in the center was a large red cake.

It looked as though there was going to be a party. But there was no one there. No one at all.

Jessie just had to have a closer look. She tiptoed through the doorway and into the room.

The first thing she noticed was that just about everything was made from things the pixie had found in the Blue Moon garden.

The table was a piece of smooth bark balanced on a stone. Arranged around it were comfortable-looking couches made from bundles of pine needles tied together with grass.

The mats that covered the table were flower

4

petals. The brown bowls were the little cups that fell from the acorns that grew on Blue Moon's big oak tree. The "plums" were blueberries. And the "cake" in the middle of the table was half a strawberry!

Jessie wandered around, looking at everything. Tucked into the pixie's hammock was a fluffy, pale gray feather. This must be the pixie's blanket.

As she stretched out a finger to touch it, she heard a scuffle in the doorway. She spun around guiltily.

A pixie was standing there, wiping his feet carefully on the doormat. He had a thin, pointed face and dark, dancing eyes. He wore brightly colored clothes and a striped cap. In his hands he was carrying a gold-wrapped parcel tied up with a piece of grass.

"You're here already, it is!" he exclaimed in a squeaky voice. "And the great red tent—you did bring it, too!" His face creased into a thousand lines as he smiled.

He bounded into the room and handed his parcel to Jessie. "Many happies," he said warmly. Then he

5

looked around. "Old Dingle? Where is he?"

"Is this . . . Old Dingle's place?" asked Jessie. She was finding it hard to take everything in.

"Of course!" said the pixie. "Old Dingle is the oldest. So he has the biggest camp when we come here from the Realm. Of course. Where is he?"

"He . . . he went to get some honey, I think," Jessie stammered. "He left a note on the door."

"Aha! So Old Dingle is not here, it is," exclaimed the pixie in excitement. "But I am here. I, Littlebreeze, am here. So you open mine giftie, now."

Jessica stared at the package she was holding.

The pixie was jumping up and down impatiently. "Yes, yes! Open! You should open mine giftie first, it is," he squeaked, nodding furiously. "Because I gave it to you first."

Jessie swallowed. "This is for me?"

"Of course!" shrieked Littlebreeze. "For your moon-day. Jessie's moon-day. Old Dingle said. We will have a party, it is. For Jessie's moon-day. Old Dingle said."

He glanced at the table and licked his lips. "With treats!" he added.

Amazed, Jessie began opening the package.

"See how I tied it, all mineself?" urged Littlebreeze, dancing around in front of her. "See the nice green tie-up, all new and soft?"

"It's lovely," Jessie agreed, pulling away the piece of grass and laying it on the table.

"And see the real, special wrapping?" Littlebreeze went on. "I have been keeping it very safe, for a special giftie." He patted the package proudly.

Jessie couldn't help smiling. The wrapping paper was a gold-colored sweet wrapper that someone must have dropped in the garden. It had been smoothed out, and polished till it shone.

"It's beautiful," she said. Carefully, so as not to tear it, she unfolded the paper. She felt quite excited. What wonderful present had Littlebreeze given her? Something strange and magical? Something he'd made himself?

Inside the package was an ordinary gold safety pin.

Jessie stared at it in silence, feeling rather disappointed. A safety pin! What sort of birthday present was that?

In the back of her mind, she heard her grandmother's voice:

*See a pin and pick it up
And all the day you'll have good luck.*

Granny always said that when she bent to pick up a pin that had fallen to the ground. Then she'd fasten the pin to whatever she was wearing, and leave it there all day. That's why Irena Bins thought Granny did up her clothes with pins.

Well, this was one pin a pixie had got to first.

Suddenly Jessie realized that Littlebreeze was watching her anxiously, waiting for thanks.

"Oh!" she cried weakly. "Oh, how wonderful. How *useful*. Just what I wanted."

EMILY RODDA

has written many books for children, including the Rowan of Rin books. She has won the Children's Book Council of Australia Book of the Year Award an unprecedented five times. A former editor, Ms. Rodda is also the best-selling author of adult mysteries under the name Jennifer Rowe. She lives in Australia.